D0624911

APR 1 5 2019

This is no longer property of King County Library System

For Elah, Arthur and Scarlett - three little cubs who love bear hugs

Jana

In memory of Mum

Kay

First published in 2017 by Child's Play (International) Ltd
Ashworth Road, Bridgemead, Swindon SN5 7YD, UK

First published in USA in 2018 by Child's Play Inc
250 Minot Avenue, Auburn, Maine 04210

Distributed in Australia by Child's Play Australia Pty Ltd
Unit 10/20 Narabang Way, Belrose, Sydney, NSW 2085

Text copyright © 2017 Jana Novotny Hunter
Illustrations copyright © 2017 Child's Play (International) Ltd
The moral rights of the author and illustrator have been asserted

All rights reserved

ISBN 978-1-84643-987-2
CLP140217CPL04179872

Printed in Shenzhen, China

1 3 5 7 9 10 8 6 4 2

A catalogue record of this book
is available from the British Library

www.childs-play.com

A
BEAR HUG
at Bedtime

Jana
Novotny Hunter

illustrated by
Kay Widdowson

KING COUNTY LIBRARY SYSTEM WA

In my jungle, there's a TIGER.
She's a **stripy**, orange tiger...

...hiding behind trees,
chasing me through
tall grasses —
ready to **pounce!**

I *run, run, run,*

over, under and through.

BUT...

...if she's *quick* and catches up,

as tigers often can...

...I stroke her fur and snuggle
up to my stripy Tiger Gran.

In my forest,
there's a MONKEY.

She's a **mischief-maker**

monkey...

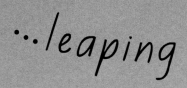

...leaping

through tall branches,
dangling by her tail –
ready to spring!

We
swing, swing, swing,

high above the trees.

BUT...

...if she **jumps** down to the ground,

the minute that she lands...

...we'll **roll around** like acrobats
and balance on our hands.

In my desert, there's a LIZARD.

He's a **cheeky**, sneaky lizard,
crawling towards me, ready to dart.

We dig, dig, dig,
and make a massive
pile of sand.

BUT...

...if I get covered
and my feet need to **wriggle**,
I poke out my toes and waggle them.

It makes my lizard **giggle!**

In my ocean,
there's a LOBSTER.

I **splash** and **kick** the water
for a lovely lobster laugh.

On my mountain, there's a BEAR.
A hungry, HAIRY bear who jumps out
from nowhere, ready to eat me!

I *climb, climb, climb,*
as fast as I can.

BUT...

...if he saves me from a **fall**,
I hold on very tight...

...and tell him he's the best bear of all, and give him...

a BEAR HUG

goodnight!